I WANT MUCH MORE THAN A

by
CHARLES BERLINER

With an INTRODUCTION by
FLORENCE HENDERSON

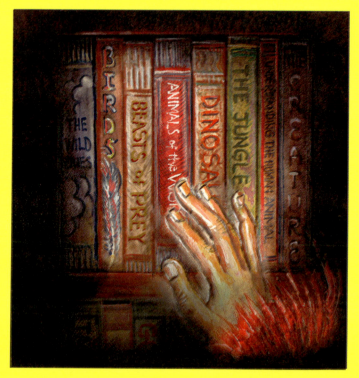

...SEARCHING FOR A DOOR TO MORE

Copyright © 2006 by Charles Berliner. 30564-BERL
Library of Congress Control Number: 2006902427
ISBN 10: Softcover 1-4257-1192-8

ISBN 13: Softcover 978-1-4257-1192-4

All rights reserved. No part of this book may be reproduced or transmitted in any form or by any means, electronic or mechanical, including photocopying, recording, or by any information storage and retrieval system, without permission in writing from the copyright owner.

This is a work of fiction. Names, characters, places and incidents either are the product of the author's imagination or are used fictitiously, and any resemblance to any actual persons, living or dead, events, or locales is entirely coincidental. This book was printed in the United States of America.

Acknowledgement is made to the book, ANIMALS, Selected by Jim Harter, published by Dover Publications, Inc., and used as the source of visual inspiration for the depiction of living animals.

It is not the author's intention to embarrass any animals by the publication of this book.

To order additional copies of this book, contact:
Xlibris Corporation
1-888-795-4274
www.Xlibris.com
Orders@Xlibris.com

AN INTRODUCTION
by
FLORENCE HENDERSON

I had the good fortune to work with Charles Berliner on two big musicals. He created the most beautiful costumes for me in *The Sound of Music* for the Los Angeles Music Center production of that show. The following year he created the most whimsical costumes for me in *Bells Are Ringing*. Charles understood my character so well.

Now, I have four grandchildren and I can't wait for them, and children of all ages, to read Charles' book. I WANT MUCH MORE THAN A DINOSAUR is creative, imaginative and humorous -- just like Charles!

AN OCTOPUS IS AN OCTOPUS

AND NOTHING MORE...

A MONKEY IS A MONKEY

AND NOTHING MORE...

AN EIGHT-LEGGED BEASTIE
IN A TREE BY THE SEA

AN ELEPHANT IS AN ELEPHANT

AND NOTHING MORE...

A KANGAROO IS A KANGAROO

AND NOTHING MORE...

A CREATURE WHO CAN HOP, SQUIRT, KICK AND FIGHT

A RABBIT IS A RABBIT

AND NOTHING MORE...

AN OWL IS AN OWL

AND NOTHING MORE...

BIG EARS, BIG EYES, FLUFFY TAIL IN THE SKY

A GIRAFFE IS A GIRAFFE

AND NOTHING MORE...

A SHARK IS A SHARK

AND NOTHING MORE...

A MEAN SPOTTED FISH
WITH ITS OWN PERISCOPE

A WOLF IS A WOLF

AND NOTHING MORE...

A FROG IS A FROG

AND NOTHING MORE...

A MOST STRANGE AND BIZARRE CROON AT THE MOON

A BEAR IS A BEAR

AND NOTHING MORE...

A SNAIL IS A SNAIL

AND NOTHING MORE...

PUT THEM TOGETHER, WHAT COMES WHEN YOU WAIT?

A HONEY-LOVER WITH A SHELL IN WHICH TO HIBERNATE

A DUCK IS A DUCK

AND NOTHING MORE...

A BEAVER IS A BEAVER

AND NOTHING MORE...

IT'S LIKE A PLATYPUS.

A PLATYPUS IS REAL!

"A Platypus is an Australian egg-laying mammal.
It has webbed feet and a duck-like bill.
It is not extinct, but is with us still!"

CHARLES BERLINER is an internationally known designer of scenery and/or costumes for plays, musicals, film, television and dance theatre. For several years he was designer for the renowned Improvisational Theatre Project at the Mark Taper Forum in Los Angeles, creating scenery and costumes for productions performed for both children and adults. One of the few recipients of an Individual Design Arts Fellowship for Theatrical Design from the National Endowment for the Arts, his multi-award-winning designs have been included in national and international exhibitions.

FURTHERMORE

Thanks to Florence Henderson for her delightful INTRODUCTION to this book. A creative inspiration to us all, audience and colleagues alike, she always gives "MORE THAN 100%" to everything with which she is involved!

If anyone asks, the boy's name is Art. This is not a nickname for Arthur. Art is named after a subject that was once always taught to students in the public school system along with "reading, writing and arithmetic."

I am fortunate to have had the guidance of my public school art teachers in San Francisco who helped to further my interest in this subject, as well as supportive, personal involvement from my late parents, Irving and Helen Berliner, who encouraged me to pursue a career in the arts.

-- Charles Berliner